Father Christmas
On His Way To
Tom's House

by Ann Bryant
edited by Alison Hedger

Illustrations by David Meldrum

A new story about Father Christmas and his journey to Tom's house on Christmas Eve.
A song with actions to the traditional chorus of Jingle Bells, plus musical games and activities, are also included.
This music book is designed to help teachers with limited or no musical experience.

The PICTURE BOOK PERCUSSION series develops structured percussion playing,
corporate speaking and listening skills.

For Jane Appleton, with love, and thanks for all your help.

Book and cover design by Chlöe Alexander.
Printed in Great Britain by Printwise (Haverhill) Limited, Suffolk.

Order No. GA11099

Welcome To This Book

Father Christmas On His Way To Tom's House is the second in the Picture Book Percussion series which helps teachers tackle percussion music with young children.

This book is fun and ideal as part of an end of term Christmas concert. Teachers do not have to be musicians to use the book successfully. Simply read the story and add the suggested sounds as shown. Do not be put off in any way should you not have a wide variety of percussion instruments to hand. With a little imagination, almost anything around the classroom can be used to create the desired effect. For instance, shaking sheets of paper, thudding on an upturned waste bin, banging a plimsoll on the floor...

This story is ideal for increasing listening skills and for cultivating an appropriate sound response. There are places for soft corporate speaking, and also speaking with a controlled increase in volume. A snore is required, and there are other places where vocal sounds could be used successfully. For example, a 'swishhhhh' for touching the tops of the pine trees. The children may also have a few ideas of their own.

Father Christmas On His Way To Tom's House can also be used as a story book. Either way, I hope you will enjoy using it again and again, year after year.

Ann Bryant

coconuts.

Suggested Instruments for the Story

COCONUT HALVES

CLAVES

CABASA

WOODBLOCK
with wooden beater

SANDBLOCKS

MARACAS

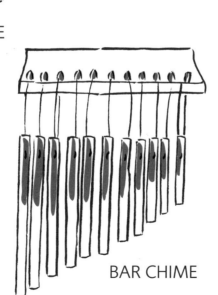

TAMBOURINE

XYLOPHONE with beater

INDIAN BELLS

BAR CHIME

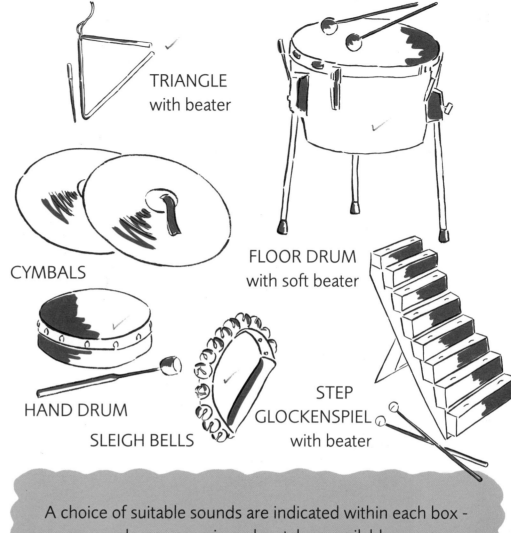

TRIANGLE
with beater

CYMBALS

FLOOR DRUM
with soft beater

HAND DRUM

SLEIGH BELLS

STEP
GLOCKENSPIEL
with beater

A choice of suitable sounds are indicated within each box - please use, mix and match as available.

The instruments shown on the story pages are suggestions: please use anything to hand that will colour the story with an appropriate sound. Alternatives made from everyday items are fun. For example, crunching of sweet papers, small stones in a sweetie tube or box, a pencil run over corrugated paper. And don't forget the noises which need no pre-preparation - body and vocal sounds.

On Christmas Eve, Father Christmas sets off with his reindeer to take presents to all the children in the world. He zooms through the sky on his sleigh, and if you listen carefully you can hear exactly where he is.

Tom was lying in bed feeling very excited, when from far away he heard

"Hoy-a-hoy!"

*All say "hoy-a-hoy!" several times,
as though far away in the distance*

7

Father Christmas was telling his reindeer to go faster.

"Hoy-a-hoy!"

"Great" thought Tom,
"Father Christmas is on his way!"

All say "Hoy-a-hoy!" a little louder than before

As Tom listened, he felt sure he could hear the reindeers' hooves galloping along.

After that, Tom definitely couldn't go to sleep. He was too busy listening to the noises of this special night.

First he heard a feathery, wispy sort of noise.

"That must be Father Christmas' sleigh brushing the tops of the tall pine trees" thought Tom.

Next Tom heard a whooshing, swirling noise.

"That must be Father Christmas whizzing up and down the snowy slopes" he thought.

xylaphone

3

As Tom listened and waited,
he heard something making a
sparkling, tinkling sound.

"That must be Father Christmas zipping
in and out of all the sparkling stars"
thought Tom. And he kept his eyes
closed to imagine the brilliant sight.

bells

After a little while Tom heard a muffly, thuddy kind of sound.

"That must be the reindeers bumping into the clouds" he thought.

Still Tom waited and listened.
The next thing he could hear
was a rattly, crashy sound.

"Father Christmas must be getting
very near" thought Tom.
"That noise must be the sleigh stopping
on top of a house near by!"

Tambarie

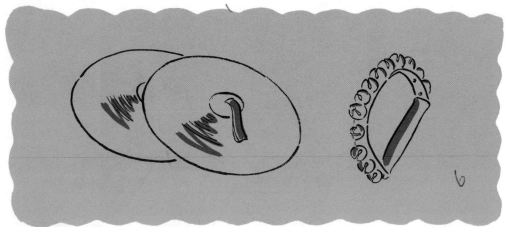

Tom sat bolt upright in bed.
He didn't move a muscle as he listened
and listened and listened.
But there was only silence...
until...

very slowly...

the bedroom door opened...

And in came his mother!
"What are you doing sitting up,
wide awake?" she said to Tom.

Then she gave him a big hug
and told him that Father Christmas
doesn't visit houses where the
children are still awake.

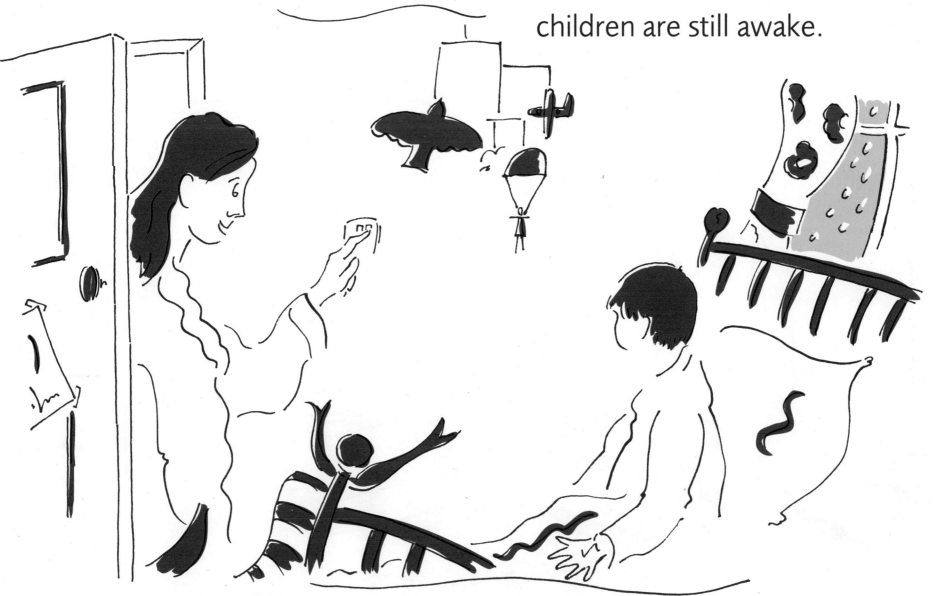

So Tom settled down under his duvet
and closed his eyes tightly,
trying really hard to go to sleep.

19

All the sounds that Tom had heard came back to him, one by one.

The reindeers' hooves...

The sleigh brushing the tops of the pine trees...

The whizzing up and down the snowy slopes...

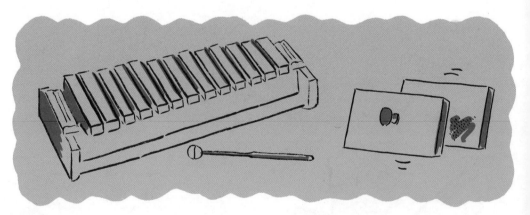

The twinkling stars...

The bumping into the clouds...

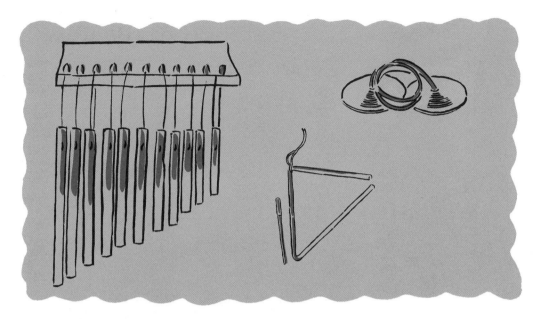

The sleigh on the roof top...

After a little while all the sounds seemed to roll into one.

It was a hazy, blurry and soft sound – as gentle as a bubble, but Tom could just still hear it.

All the instruments in the story played very, very quietly

At last Tom went to sleep!

The next morning Tom raced downstairs holding his stocking.

"Happy Christmas Mum. Happy Christmas Dad.
Happy Christmas Benny."
(That was Tom's baby brother.)
Together they opened all their presents
and there was a great tearing and
crinkling, wrinkling and ripping!

All the instruments played loudly

Tom loved all his presents and he
thought of Father Christmas.

"Thank you" he whispered.
"I hope you're having
a good sleep now."

Father Christmas certainly was!
In fact, if you listen very carefully
you can even hear him snoring…

All snore!

It's Christmas Eve

A song to the chorus music of Jingle Bells.
You may like to add the sounds as used in the story.

1 Christmas Eve, Christmas Eve,
Santa's on his way,
Brushing all the tree tops
With his reindeer and his sleigh. It's
Christmas Eve, Christmas Eve,
Santa's on his way,
Brushing all the tree tops
With his reindeer and his sleigh.

(Then as above but replace lines 3 and 7 with the following)

2 *Whizzing down the ski slopes...*

3 *Zipping through the starlight...*

4 *Bumping into snow clouds...*

5 *Landing on the roof tops...*

Actions To Go With The Song

Repeat the following, each time it comes:

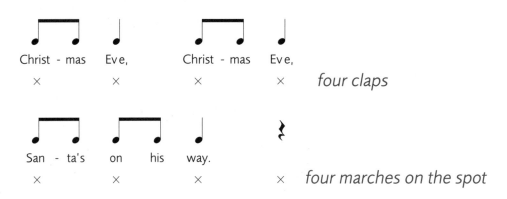

and vary the actions for the remainder of each verse as follows:

1 Stretch up tall like a pine tree and sway quickly from side to side

2 Hold ski poles and ski in time with the beat

3 Skip in own little circle

4 Punch in front with alternate hands

5 Small bounces

Activities And Games

Christmas Signals

The children need to know what actions to do when they hear you playing the following musical instruments:

COCONUT HALVES
Hands on head with fingers spread like reindeer antlers

MARACAS
Standing tall and thin like a pine tree

TRIANGLE
Pointing to stars

SLEIGH BELLS
Hands on hips mimicking a hearty Father Christmas laugh

XYLOPHONE GLISSANDO (descending)
Pretend to ski

When you play one of the instruments, the children have to respond by making the appropriate signal.
Anyone who gets it wrong or is late, is out.

Spot The Corner

Designate each corner of your room to one of the following.
A picture or symbol may make this clearer to the children.

Father Christmas coming down on a roof top

The sleigh brushing past the tree tops

Tom sitting on the bed

The sleigh dancing in and out of the stars

Devise four simple melodic phrases, each of five notes, to represent the picture or symbol of the four corners. For example, the first one could be five descending notes (G, F, E, D, C). The second could be five repeated notes (G, G, G, G, G), the third 5 ascending notes (C, D, E, F, G) and the fourth a melody with skips in it (C, E, D, F, E).

The children must become familiar with each melody and learn which corner it refers to. Then they stand up, and you play any of the melodies. The children have to recognise which one you are playing, and run to the appropriate part of the room! This activity may also be played as an elimination game.

Father Christmas Says...

This is a seasonal variation of the well-known children's elimination game 'Simon says...'

You say "Father Christmas says..." and the children must do what you say. Keep the speed of change rapid, and then just pop in an instruction leaving out "Father Christmas says". Those children who do the action without "Father Christmas says" are out.

You will no doubt have ideas of your own, but how about including:

Waggle your antlers

Fill up your sack

Be a star

Be a Christmas tree

Drive the reindeer